WRITTEN BY
JULIA DONALDSON

ILLUSTRATED BY
AXEL SCHEFFLER

THE GRUFFALO'S CHILD

MACMILLAN CHILDREN'S BOOKS

The Gruffalo said that no gruffalo should
Ever set foot in the deep dark wood.
"Why not? Why not?" *"Because if you do
The Big Bad Mouse will be after you.
I met him once,"* said the Gruffalo.
"I met him a long long time ago."

"What does he look like? Tell us, Dad.
Is he terribly big and terribly bad?"

"*I can't quite remember,*" the Gruffalo said.
Then he thought for a minute and scratched his head.

"The Big Bad Mouse is terribly strong
And his scaly tail is terribly long.

His eyes are like pools of terrible fire
And his terrible whiskers are tougher than wire."

One snowy night when the Gruffalo snored
The Gruffalo's Child was feeling bored.

The Gruffalo's Child was feeling brave
So she tiptoed out of the gruffalo cave.
The snow fell fast and the wind blew wild.
Into the wood went the Gruffalo's Child.

Aha! Oho! A trail in the snow!
Whose is this trail and where does it go?
A tail poked out of a logpile house.
Could this be the tail of the Big Bad Mouse?

Out slid the creature. His eyes were small
And he didn't have whiskers – no, none at all.

"You're not the Mouse." *"Not I,"* said the snake.
"He's down by the lake – eating gruffalo cake."

The snow fell fast and the wind blew wild.
"I'm not scared," said the Gruffalo's Child.

Aha! Oho! Marks in the snow!
Whose are these claw marks? Where do they go?
Two eyes gleamed out of a treetop house.
Could these be the eyes of the Big Bad Mouse?

Down flew the creature. His tail was short
And he didn't have whiskers of any sort.

"You're not the Mouse." *"Toowhoo, not I,*
But he's somewhere nearby, eating gruffalo pie."

The snow fell fast and the wind blew wild.
"I'm not scared," said the Gruffalo's Child.

Aha! Oho! A track in the snow!
Whose is this track and where does it go?
Whiskers at last! And an underground house!
Could this be the home of the Big Bad Mouse?

Out slunk the creature. His eyes weren't fiery.
His tail wasn't scaly. His whiskers weren't wiry.

"You're not the Mouse."   *"Oh no, not me.*
He's under a tree – drinking gruffalo tea."

"It's all a trick!" said the Gruffalo's Child
As she sat on a stump where the snow lay piled.
"I don't *believe* in the Big Bad Mouse . . .

"But here comes a little one, out of his house!
Not big, not bad, but a mouse at least –
You'll taste good as a midnight feast."

"Wait!" said the mouse. "Before you eat,
There's a friend of mine that you ought to meet.
If you'll let me hop onto a hazel twig
I'll beckon my friend so bad and big."

The Gruffalo's Child unclenched her fist.
"The Big Bad Mouse – so he *does* exist!"
The mouse hopped into the hazel tree.
He beckoned, then said, *"Just wait and see."*

Out came the moon. It was bright and round.
A terrible shadow fell onto the ground.

Who is this creature so big, bad and strong?
His tail and his whiskers are terribly long.
His ears are enormous, and over his shoulder
He carries a nut as big as a boulder!

"The Big Bad Mouse!" yelled the Gruffalo's Child.
The mouse jumped down from the twig and smiled.

Aha! Oho! Prints in the snow.

Whose are these footprints? Where do they go?

The footprints led to the gruffalo cave

Where the Gruffalo's Child was a bit less brave.

The Gruffalo's Child was a bit less bored . . .

And the Gruffalo snored
and snored and snored.

For Franzeska – J.D.
For Freya and Cora – A.S.

First published 2004 by Macmillan Children's Books
This edition published 2016 by Macmillan Children's Books
an imprint of Pan Macmillan
20 New Wharf Road, London N1 9RR
Associated companies throughout the world
www.panmacmillan.com

ISBN 978-1-5098-0476-4

A CIP catalogue record for this book is available
from the British Library.

Printed in China